The Hug-A-Lump

Written by: Brenda Brooks

Illustrated by: Emily-Anne Guiry

Print information available on the last page

Rev. date: 06/21/2019

To order additional copies of this book, contact:
Xlibris
1-888-795-4274
www.Xlibris.com
Orders@Xlibris.com

I sat up in bed, I rubbed my eyes, and then I shook my head.

A who's-it, a what's-it, an I-don't-know it was sitting on my bed.

I saw a note pinned to
it's chest and thought
that I should see

Exactly what this

thing-a-ma-jig had

to say to me.

Hi my name is
Hug-A-Lump and
I am here for you.
When you feel sad or
mad or scared, just take
a-hold of me.

Squeeze me tight with
all your might and
whisper 1, 2, 3
And I will pass a gift
to you; I promise,
wait and see!!

I quickly dressed;
I ran downstairs,
because oh by golly gee!

My Hug-A-Lump,
my newfound friend,
my parents had to see.

We went outside to play
awhile and there

I skinned my knee.

It hurt so bad, I cried

and cried, and mommy

came for me.

She said we had to clean
it so better it would be.

Oh Hug-A-Lump I really
need the gift you
promised me.

I hugged him hard and
held him close and
whispered 1, 2, 3

Oh my, what's this,
could it really be

That as I finished saying
three my mommy was
done with my knee.

We went to school,
they changed my class;
they changed my teacher
too I was so scared,
I knew no one;
what was I to do?

Oh Hug-A-Lump again
I need the gift you
promised me.

I hugged him hard and
held him close and
whispered 1, 2, 3
vh my, what's this,
could it really be
Someone is speaking,
asking me to be their
friend, whoopee!!

Hug-A-Lump,
I know your gift,
it came to me today!

That hugging seems
to be a way of making
some things A-OK.

So I will hug my
mom and dad;
I'll hug my kitty too
But most of all my

Hug-A-Lump,
I'll keep on hugging you.

Printed in the United States
By Bookmasters